Rob Do
In This Skull Hotel Wh
A Killian Turne

Texts accompanying an installation
recreating Killian Turner's last
known residence in Neukölln,
West Berlin, 1983–1985

Broken Dimanche Press

There was a stove, a pot, a pan, a few cups and plates, a desk, a bed. Apart from that, the only things he had were books.

– Sarah Flanagan on Killian Turner

To the memory of Jean-Pierre Passolet

TABLE OF CONTENTS

Following page: A facsimile from Turner's copy of Jean Genet's *The Thief's Journal*, which he heavily annotated. Turner filled the books he owned with extensive notes and marginalia, which some have suggested add up to a work of literature themselves. In this instance, Turner writes: 'Prison of a mind gone awry, to a place neither of us could call home exactly, but where the love of absence, ex nihilo, exists all joy is void, all presence null, the point of disappearing is to say: I have never existed at all & I don't pretend to play at your games. Your literature is not my literature, your morals are not my morals. My home is void.' — RD sky its lonely flight. I could have told of my past life in another tone, in other words. I have made it sound heroic because I have within me what is needed to do so, lyricism. My concern for coherence makes it my duty to carry on my adventure in the *tone* of my book. It will have served to define the indications which my *past presents*; I have laid my finger, heavily and many times, on poverty and punished crime. It is toward these that I shall go. Not with the premeditated intention of finding them, in the manner of Catholic saints, but slowly, without trying to evade the fatigues and horrors of the venture.

But am I being clear? It is not a matter of applying a philosophy of unhappiness. Quite the contrary. The prison – let us name that place in both the world and the mind – toward which I go offers me more joys than your honours and festivals. Nevertheless, it is these which I shall seek. I aspire to your recognition, your consecration.

Heroized, my book, which has become my Genesis, contains – should contain – the commandments which I cannot transgress. If I am worthy of it, it will reserve for me the infamous glory of which it is the great master, for to what shall I refer if not to it? And, purely from the viewpoint of a more commonplace morality, would it not be logical for this book to draw my body on and lure me to prison? Not, may I point out, through some swift procedure governed by your principles, but by means of a fatality contained within it, which I have put there, and which, as I have intended, keeps me as witness, field of experimentation and living proof of its virtue and my responsibility.

I wish to speak of these prison festivals. The surrounding presence of wounded males is already a blessing that is granted me. However, I mention this in passing; other situations (the army, sport, etc.) can offer me a similar one. In the second volume of this *Journal*, which will be called *Morals Charge*, I intend to report, describe and comment upon the festivals of an inner prison that I discover within me after going through the region of myself which I have called Spain.

PREFACE
Rob Doyle

Much has been written – too much, perhaps – about the West Berlin of the 1970s and '80s – that decadent, post-punk, bohemian city where Iggy Pop and David Bowie got clean; where Blixa Bargeld bashed bricks against sheets of metal and created Einstürzende Neubauten; where beautiful ghouls fucked and danced in the shadow of the Wall, amid the post-war desolation of Neukölln and Kreuzberg. Yet what makes Berlin so vital a city is its fierce refusal of nostalgia, of being hindered by too great a respect for the past. This is a city where the present is a perpetual, volatile experiment; where art, youth culture, and technology acquire velocity from the gravitational pull of the future. Today, Berlin's pulse is the beat of techno, and whatever Europe is mutating into may well emerge from the city's underworld of political ferment, gender and sexual experimentation, and creative unrest.

And yet, the ghosts of the past continue to haunt the city – ghosts of terror, catastrophe and collective insanity. One of Berlin's ghosts is Killian Turner, the Irish writer to whom this book and accompanying installation pay tribute. The biographical facts of Turner's strange life can be read in my essay included here, 'Exiled in the Infinite – Killian

Turner, Ireland's Vanished Literary Outlaw', which was first published in *The Moth* magazine and later included in my book *This Is the Ritual*. To my surprise, that essay helped stir up a renewed interest in Turner's life and work which shows no signs of abating.[1] Turner's rediscovery – if that is not too strong a word – coincided with the much publicised 'boom' in Irish literature: the emergence of a generation of writers impatient with the staid conventions of Irish fiction. To this new wave, Killian Turner has become a totemic figure, symbolising creative daring, cosmopolitanism, and intellectual sweep. 'Some are born posthumously', wrote Friedrich Nietzsche. Killian Turner's obscurity in his own time, and his subsequent embrace by a later generation of writers, affirms the truth in the adage.

Turner was born in Dublin in 1948, and he disappeared in West Berlin in 1985, having left behind a singular, at times deeply disquieting body of work. In all probability, Turner took his own life. The fact that his body was never found, and the weird and sinister events that preceded his disappearance, have led to inevitable conspiracy theories, and persistent rumours that Turner is still alive. Sightings of Turner have been reported in places as far afield as Marrakech, Bali, Kandahar, and New Mexico.

---

1 For all its unexpected impact, my essay was not without its detractors. Mark Blacklock, for instance, wrote in *The Guardian*, 'Anything on Turner is always welcome, so difficult to access are his works, but this biographical account doesn't get us much closer to the real thing.'

London Review Bookshop
14 Bury Place
London
WC1A 2JL
020 7269 9030
books@lrbshop.co.uk
www.lrbshop.co.uk

342 1553 84

Four Soldiers	£12.99
A Meal in Winter	£7.99
In This Skull Hotel Where I Ne	£10.00
Magazine	£6.00

Number of Items: 4

Subtotal.   £36.98

Total.   £36.98

Payment
Cash:	£40.00
Change:	£3.02

Thank you for your custom.

----- VAT SUMMARY -----

Vat @ 20%.   £0.00

Date   12-Oct-2018 13:58:07
Receipt   264,465

Like many of Ireland's writers, Turner produced much of his work abroad. The literary peers among which he belongs are generally not Irish. He has far more in common with a purveyor of philosophically sophisticated science-fiction like Philip K Dick, or with the mystical ecstasies of Clarice Lispector, than he does with, say, John McGahern or Maeve Brennan.

The burgeoning field of Turner scholarship has produced some fascinating work. Dr. Gillian Lund at Birkbeck University recently gave a thrilling talk on the influence of psychedelic drugs in Turner's work, placing him in a lineage of Western artists influenced by shamanic and psychedelic cultures which includes Baudelaire, Artaud, Burroughs and Terence McKenna. Dr. Lund convincingly argued that a single experience with the drug DMT in 1981 effected a radical shift in Turner's metaphysical and cosmological outlook, which in turn influenced the nature of his subsequent literary work. Personally, I would be delighted to read a thorough analysis of the relationship between Turner's *oeuvre* and the Gnostic and mystical traditions with which he was intimately familiar. The influence of Buddhist and Hindu philosophy on Turner's writing is another potentially fruitful area of investigation.

Here in Germany, a number of academics have explored the implications for queer theory in Turner's transgressive and pornographic Berlin writings. Turner's complicated homosexuality, and his misogynistic – indeed, femicidal – tendencies have led some to express reservations about his growing acclaim (let it not be forgotten that Turner once called, however ironically, for nothing less than 'a Final Solution to the female question', and for 'the atrocity of creating life to be punishable by death'). Turner's enthusiasm for anti-male texts like Valerie Solanas' *SCUM Manifesto,* however, complicate attempts to write him off as a straightforward misogynist. It is perhaps more accurate to describe Turner as a sort of gender-anarchist, who employed shock tactics to destabilise traditional gender categories.

For the series *a book, a room* to which this volume belongs, we have recreated Killian Turner's last known place of residence – the apartment in Neukölln where he lived until his disappearance – at Büro BDP, the premises of the publishing house Broken Dimanche Press, also located in Neukölln. As in Turner's haunting 'House Sequence', it is hoped that the experience of encountering Turner's work in a setting which replicates his final home, a portal might be opened onto what Turner called 'All-Time-Now' - an imaginative, abyssal zone that exists beyond time and space, where 'good and evil are one, are nothing.'

— Rob Doyle, Neukölln, January 2018

14

EXILED IN THE INFINITE – KILLIAN TURNER, IRELAND'S VANISHED LITERARY OUTLAW
Rob Doyle

It is impossible today to read either the work or the life of the novelist, essayist, epigrammatist and pornographer, Killian Turner, without seeking in it clues to the mystery of his disappearance, or attempting to locate the genesis of the strange obsessions that would eventually consume him.

There is little beyond what Turner called 'the crash-landing site of my birthplace' by which he could meaningfully be called an 'Irish writer.' In fact, his body of work, taken as a whole, might be seen as Turner's lifelong project of effacing all marks of nationhood from his authorial voice and literary being. It is clear from comments made by Turner in his letters to other writers and artists (the majority of them obscure), and certain remarks in his essays[2], that, like such pointedly un-Irish compatriot-predecessors as Beckett and Joyce, Turner wished to be considered first and foremost a European author.[3]

---

2 For instance: 'Why should it be that, in an age of burgeoning communication technologies which render physical space and geographical difference increasingly insignificant, a writer, or any artist, must continue to be categorised primarily in reference to his *national* peers and forebears? It is obvious to me that... writers should from henceforth be categorised according to affinities of style, areas of inquiry and formal concerns, rather than by the comparatively inexpressive fact of their birth-proximity to other writers.' *(Erased Horizons, Forgotten Shores: Essays 1975–1982*, pg 103, Sacrum Press, Ireland)

3 Turner's shedding of his national identity undoubtedly had a stimulating effect on the development

Born into an upper-middle class family in Dalkey, county Dublin, in 1948, Turner only began writing with any seriousness in his early twenties.[4] It may be that Turner was prevented from writing as a younger man by the unhappiness of his home life. Maureen Turner, Killian's mother, died after complications resulting from the birth of her only child. Killian's father, Henry, was a history teacher in a private secondary school in Dalkey, and a man of trenchantly melancholy disposition. In the smog-choked winter evenings of Killian's boyhood and adolescence, Henry would call his son into his study. There, as Killian stood silently by his side, the father would issue sweeping utterances about the destruction inherent in the very cells of civilisation, the transience of mankind, and the utter folly of all our humanistic dreams of progress, peace and salvation. Both astronomy and archaeology, declared father to son, betray the appalling truth of our place in the universe as an accidental

---

of his art. Shorn of the parochial concerns which predominate in the work of many Irish writers of his generation, Turner was freed to soar outwards and away from the homeland, towards universal or exotic themes. In a famous essay, Jorge Luis Borges expresses frustration at Argentinian authors' unreflecting attachment to *place* in their work; seeing themselves primarily as Argentinian writers, they crowd their stories with local colour and thematic content that caters to the literary sightseer and tourist. Yet why, asks Borges, should an Argentinean writer not eschew the constraining tropes of locational realism, and take as his subject the universe itself? Just as Borges met his own challenge, revolutionising the short story by engineering sublimely playful, metaphysical mysteries and ingenious hoax-narratives, so too did Killian Turner explode prejudices about what 'Irish literature' was allowed to do, grappling as he did with ideas of reckless scope and ambition: time, infinity, chaos, Nazism, nuclear war, sex, evil, and language itself (conceived as a malign and relentless viral weapon, of origin foul but obscure).

4 At twenty-four he published his first short story, in a Trinity College journal. 'Father Coward' is the confessional monologue of a north Dublin priest who secretly harbours heretical notions concerning the true, chilling significance of the visions at Fatima.

and fear-crazed species, rubbing its bleary eyes to find itself perched aboard a rock that hurtles through black infinities, whose only destiny is to be swallowed up once more in the great darkness. Religion, morality, truth, human solidarity – these are nothing, proclaimed the father, but the consoling fictions bred by our proximity to the abyss and the panic it engenders.

It can only be imagined what impression these dark lessons had on the sensitive young Killian. What we can be sure of, however, is that the great, seismic event of Turner's youth was the suicide by poisoning of Henry Turner at the age of fifty-three, when Killian was eighteen. This event, reappearing in various guises, is the black hole, the vortex of destructive fury around which Turner's writing orbits, drawing ever closer, inviting - and this is what gives the experience of reading Turner what has been called its 'vertiginous', 'abyssal' quality – a kind of cosmic-orgasmic catastrophe in the psyche of both reader and writer, intended to eclipse the original trauma of the suicide.

Until the death of his father, Turner seems to have been a rather normal child and young man. He enjoyed hurling, soccer and GAA. His schoolmates and friends recalled him as being quiet, but devastatingly witty when called upon to use his wit as a weapon, and gently hilarious when among friendlier company. He was something of a loner by disposition, yet not unpopular. Beginning in early childhood, Turner read voraciously. In his teens he had a colossal appetite for science fiction and so-called 'weird' fiction (his fascination with the work of HP Lovecraft bordered on the religious: the young Turner would spend whole weekends in his room, drawing wildly imaginative pictures of the Old Ones of Lovecraftian mythology, and not infrequently his father and any visitors to the household would be startled by sudden, bellowed recitals, issuing from Killian's bedroom, of the incantations of savage tribes to their hellish gods familiar to readers of Lovecraft's stories: *C'thriu nazzgath! He'krtarral Nephazzatam! Kaheebiz Abascciss!*)

In his late teens and early twenties, Turner lived on the inheritance he had received upon his father's death. He did not pursue third level studies, though he did continue to read as much, and more widely than ever, nourishing keen interests in mythology, anthropology, and avant-garde physics. It was during this period that Turner began to imagine he could become a writer. At the age of twenty-five, having published two short stories and several reviews in various Irish publications, he set to work on his first novel. *Edge of Voices* took four years to complete, and a further two to find a publisher, finally seeing print when its author was thirty-one. Regarded from its first appearance as one of the true oddities of Irish literature (a literature hardly scarce of oddities), the novel is equal parts semi-autobiographical portrayal of an unremarkable Dublin adolescence, and fantastical, eerie missive from the furthermost extremes of human experience. The story, such as it is, tells of a boy, Michael Kavanagh, similar in most ways to Turner, who, on the day of his Catholic confirmation, begins to receive, or believe he is receiving, telepathic messages from a hyper-intelligent presence, perhaps extraterrestrial or even inter-dimensional in origin, which may once have inhabited the earth in corporeal form, but now exists only as an imperceptible atmospheric layer. Michael is deeply troubled by the messages, often doubting his own sanity. Yet he continues to live his outward life more or less as usual, enduring the timeless trials of adolescence and winning local renown as a full-back on the under-17 GAA team. Then, after Michael reaches his eighteenth birthday, loses his virginity (in what must rank as one of the most hilarious love scenes in Irish fiction) and applies to study European History at Trinity College, all in the same bittersweet week, the transmissions abruptly stop, never to resume. The final sixty pages of the book are given over to an exegesis, supposedly set down in the fourth millennium AD, of the messages received by Michael over a three-year period during his adolescence. The implication seems to be that

Michael has become some sort of messiah, or the founder of a new religion or civilisation.

Edge of Voices was first published not in Ireland but in France, and then in New York, by small independent publishers committed to the literary heterodox. Turner gave several readings in Paris, where he gained minor cult status. Then, when he was thirty-three, he received an Irish Arts Council bursary, which he used to fund a trip around Europe. He travelled for three months, filling several notebooks with reflections on Post-War Europe that were to inform his work for years to come. Instead of returning to Ireland after his travels, Turner settled in West Berlin, where he was to remain for the final three years prior to his disappearance.

Throughout the early 80s, from the anarchist and bohemian neighbourhood of Neukölln he had made his home, Turner continued to send stories, essays and other, increasingly uncategorisable writings almost exclusively to Irish journals, as if still engaged in a dialogue with a land he had otherwise repudiated. (By no means all of these pieces were accepted for publication.) Turner rented a small apartment in a block largely occupied by political radicals and artists, and seemed to thrive in this environment. The poet Sarah Flanagan, who also lived in Berlin around this time and befriended Turner, later remarked that his apartment had something of the monk's cell to it. 'There was a stove, a pot, a pan, a few cups and plates, a desk, and a bed. Apart from that, the only things he had were books', she said. Asked about Turner's social and romantic life in this period, she replied: 'I don't know what to say about that. I mean, for sure he was handsome, and he had a certain charisma. But there was a... a kind of privacy to him that went beyond simple introspectiveness. Like he would only let you come so far, and then he'd step out into the grounds of the castle to meet with you. He was never unfriendly, never cold. But there was a boundary. I used to wonder about his love life. He never told me about it, and when I asked he was always wittily evasive. Later, of course, there were all the rumours, but I didn't know him any more by that stage... I used to tell him he looked like Michel Foucault, with the bald head, the intense eyes, the glasses. He liked that. He rarely laughed, but he had a lively, faint kind of smile. I remember that.'

Living within sight of the Berlin Wall, steeped in the atmosphere of what he called 'the city on earth that has come closest to the core of the darkness, hearing the very beat of the devil's wing', Turner's lifelong fascination with Nazi Germany, the Holocaust and the Second World War found endless stimulation. He took long, aimless walks through the city, at all times of day or night, overcome with visions of the enormity which had been perpetrated there mere decades ago. Reading deeply from the literature of the War, Turner developed what he described as a 'merciless obsession' with Hitler's plan, devised during the height of the Third Reich's reach and ambition, to convert the island of Ireland into the 'granary of Europe' following the final triumph of Nazism. Turner's second book, *The Garden*, was the controversial fruit of this obsession.

Coining the term 'Nazi-pastoral' to describe an almost aggressively uncategorisable work, critics were not quite sure how seriously to take its plotless, meticulously realised, seemingly deadpan 457-page portrait of an alternative, Nazified Ireland in which Hitler's plan has come to pass. Written in a documentary style recalling sociological surveys and governmental reports, *The Garden* was, according to one critic, 'either a joke in questionable taste, or the nostalgic, vindictive fantasy of a confused and lonely man, whose bitterness has bred a disingenuous sympathy for the Nazis and for Hitler.' Indeed, defenders of the book who insisted it was an extended exercise in cautionary irony, foundered when they tried to explain away the all-too-convincing sincerity in Turner's depictions of a bucolic Ireland run by communities of agrarian fascists, where cheery colleens Irish-dance around swastikas, and boys in the Hitler Youth of Ireland (whose honorary president is WB Yeats) are taught to hunt, cook and swim, whilst having their imaginations fed by Celtic and Nordic mythology, and receiving lessons in the rudiments of Darwinism and race-theory.

Thus far, sexuality had had a somewhat muted presence in Turner's work. Turner himself appears to have always been at ease with his own homosexuality (or strong homosexual tendencies), even if he was reluctant to publicise it in the conservatively Catholic Ireland where he had come of age. In Berlin, however, Turner took full advantage of the city's fierce permissiveness to explore this sexuality in a deeper way than had been possible hitherto. The discoveries he made in the course of these explorations, based on his writings subsequent to *The Garden*, were strange and disturbing, hinting at the darkest recesses of the Sadean imagination. 'It was as if', writes one of Turner's most perceptive and sympathetic critics, '[he] came to view his sexuality, and beyond that, the broader configuration of his instinctual drives, as a kind of map or diagram in which he could discern, in microcosm, all the horrors and psychopathology – political, social, personal – of the traumatic century into which he had been born.'[5]

Abandoning the last vestiges of conventional narrative fiction, and taking as his new literary models Bataille[6], Sade and Burroughs, Turner

5 Thomas Duddy, *Bludgeoning the Muse - the Transgressive Anti-Fiction of Killian Turner,* Review of Contemporary Literature, Issue 68, June 2002

6 For a period, Turner even seems to have entertained the belief that he himself was the reincarnation

ventured into murky, often questionable artistic territories. At the same time, and with equal conviction, he conducted countless nocturnal forays into Berlin's transgressive, erotic underworld. His most grotesque or bizarre adventures found their way into the writings of this period - writings which convey the unholy, anarchic allure of the Berlin night, in pages crowded with masochistic dog-men, dungeon-crawling 'spiritual abortions', bald women draped in chains 'with vaginas in their armpits and armpits in their vaginas', weeping teenage prostitutes from the Soviet hinterlands, and mute rent-boys with pure and sorrowful visages.

By this time, Turner had learned German well enough to hold a series of unglamorous jobs in Berlin (he was not making nearly enough from his writing to live off it). He worked for a time as a night-watchman on building sites on the fringes of the city. Then he got a job as a caterer on trains connecting West Berlin to various cities to the north. In one of his most difficult passages, Turner writes of the strange happiness he experienced in this job, peering out the windows at 'the silent dream of passing German landscape, a sublimely dreary post-industrial idyll whose every inch sang

---

of Bataille: 'Not figuratively, but in the full meaning of spirit recast, power enfleshed... There are nights when, woken by the howl of a junkie down in KanalStraße or the rattle of a late U-Bahn train, I walk to the darkened mirror, and from it peer the radiant, saintly eyes of Georges Bataille.' *(Visions of Cosmic Squalor / The Upheaval*, pg 90, Anti-Matter, London) However, as Bataille lived until 1962, and was therefore Turner's contemporary for fourteen years, it is difficult to understand how Turner even considered holding this eccentric notion.

of holocaust – of the holocaust already passed and the holocausts to come, for all infinity, an eternal recurrence of this most perfect human exaltation and nightmare, the ecstatic vision of an engineered hell... And then I would interrupt my window-gazing reveries and, suffused with a world-embracing love like that described by the mystics, serve Coca Cola, Pepsi, and ham sandwiches to beautiful German children and their waddling parents.'[7]

It is at this point that a heavier fog descends on the biographical trail; fact, fiction and hallucination become impossible to separate. Most of what follows cannot therefore be verified as factual truth, having been pieced together from Turner's always perilous later writings, and the sparse accounts of those who knew him at the time. It is entirely possible that most of what is here recounted bears no relation to events that took place in external reality. However, it is the author's belief that

7 Admittedly, while all of the late Turner is challenging, some of the fragmentary work of his final years, especially certain of the pieces collected in *Visions of Cosmic Squalor / The Upheaval*, can only be described as unhinged. And yet, even the most aberrant of his work has a quality of dazzling entertainment. Consider the sprawling, unfinished essay, worked on during the early eighties and unpublished at the time of his disappearance, in which Turner asserts that Joyce's final novel, the monstrous and baffling *Finnegans Wake*, is nothing less than a coded transmission intended to trigger the apocalypse. According to Turner (and this has been ridiculed by the few scholars who have bothered to address the issue at all), while Joyce was living in Trieste, he was contacted by a sinister group of Kabbalistic Jews who, given impetus by the events of World War One, were promulgating an aggressively eschatological doctrine in which language itself figured as a kind of super-weapon, radiating metaphysical contaminants through the media of literature, radio and cinema. Joyce, writes Turner, most likely considered the conspiring Kabbalists as nothing more than a picturesque nuisance. However, he goes on, the Kabbalists submitted an unwitting Joyce to a refined form of hypnotism, implanting him with the apocalyptic codes, syntactic rhythms and linguistic motifs which their ancient studies had revealed to them as the ammunition of cosmic disarray - and which, according to Turner, were to surface, unbeknownst to Joyce, across the expansive tapestry of his most mystifying novel.

what follows is, at least, an approximation of the reality that pertained within the troubled psyche of Killian Turner in the period leading to the autumn of 1985. The only events which undoubtedly did take place are those of Turner's disappearance and the subsequent investigation; the rest must be considered either metaphor or speculation.

In November or December of 1984, Turner agreed to collaborate on an industrial-noise track with a musician friend, Heinrich Mannheim, who he knew through the S/M scene. Mannheim's band, Sublime Ascent, were at the extreme end of the thriving noise-music scene in Berlin in the 80s, taking their cue from bands like Whitehouse, whose aesthetic of extreme violence and sexual cruelty Mannheim admired as being the only cultural form immune to assimilation by the capitalist-consumer system, whose primary ideological function, Mannheim believed, was to render all artistic and political acts harmless and tractable. Sublime Ascent are reported to have incorporated images and video footage of war atrocities, executions and torture into their infrequent live performances. It has even been rumoured that, in one extremely secretive performance in a disused governmental premises on the fringes of either Frankfurt or Dresden, the band improvised a set to the prolonged, ritualistic killing of a consenting and ecstatic male, hands bound and on his knees, a series of cuts made on his naked torso.

The tapes said to have resulted from the collaboration between Sublime Ascent and Killian Turner have become the holy grail of Turner aficionados. On the recordings, Turner is thought to have read from a collage made up of his own texts and those of Georges Bataille, possibly spliced with certain passages from Sade and Nietzsche, and transcripts of the commentary from the 1982 World Cup. He read over a sprawling sound-texture that lurched between extreme noise and eerie, dark-ambient sonic wasteland, performed live by Sublime Ascent. Present at the recording was a forty-something man with long, greying hair and a bushy, black moustache who was never to be seen without his wraparound sunglasses, his overall appearance suggesting a somewhat seedier Carlos Santana. This was the figure Turner would refer to in his writings sometimes as Frank Lonely, but more often as Mother D. After watching the recording session whilst drinking several cups of herbal tea, Frank Lonely/Mother D remarked that he admired the text that Turner had read, or at least what he had understood of it (his English was imperfect), and thought he had recognised certain phrases from Georges Bataille. When the day's recording was finished, the two men went out for a drink and ended up talking long into the night - about art, music, love and politics. Turner eventually stumbled back to his Neukölln apartment as a murky dawn broke over Berlin, rarely in his life having laughed or enjoyed himself so much.

The diaries Turner kept in the months immediately preceding his disappearance detail his intense, at times all-consuming friendship with Mother D. The two men shared a love for Bataille, for underground American rock bands like Suicide and Big Black, and, bizarrely, for all varieties of animated film, but especially those produced by the Disney corporation. Turner and Mother D would spend their weekends visiting cinemas all over the city, watching Bambi, The Jungle Book, Snow White and the Seven Dwarves, and whatever other feature-length cartoons they could find (they appear to have had no interest in shorter fare, such as animated TV series). 'In the presence of Mother D I re-embody the child I never truly was', wrote Turner, 'Which in turn prepares me, spiritually if not fizzically [sic] for what is to come, i.e. the great radiance / the crossing / the sacred blah-blah-blah'.[8]

It was towards the end of July that Mother D introduced Turner to a friend and ex-lover of his named Anashka. Turner was instantly enthralled. Indeed, Anashka seems to have been a formidable figure, of no great beauty, perhaps, but with intense erotic allure. Born to a Russian mother in exile

---

8 A certain lightness of tone, unusual in Turner's work, can be detected in passages and diary entries written during these months, as if the happiness inspired by his friendship with Mother D could not but seep through into Turner's authorial voice.

from the Soviet Union, and an Italian anarchist father, Anashka always wore a black beret and tight black jeans, though the rest of her apparel varied wildly. 'The beret and jeans were the frame,' wrote Turner, 'The rest was the whirring reel... of a film I could watch forever.' Anashka was twenty-nine and co-ran a gallery and performance space in Kreuzberg. She was also an artist who used the medium of dance, often augmented with vitriolic spoken-word outbursts and even, when the chemistry of a performance demanded it, physical assaults on her audience. One night she performed to an audience consisting solely of Turner, in an apartment borrowed from a friend who was visiting Poland. Turner was transfixed by the dance, which consisted for the most part of Anashka standing deathly still, wincing very occasionally, and emitting long, alarming shrieks even more infrequently. After almost three hours, Anashka collapsed to the floor and announced that the performance had concluded. Turner thanked her and asked her what the piece was called. Anashka thought about this for quite some time, before replying, *Jack Ruby and Lee Harvey Oswald*. Turner and Anashka then made love on the floor of the apartment – an experience which astonished Turner. He was to write at length about this incident on several occasions, as if trying to coax out its core meaning by approaching it from multiple angles. 'I cannot say', he concluded, 'whether the carnal fusion with Anashka was the greatest bliss of my life... or the deepest horror.'

The day after Anashka's performance, Mother D told Turner of an abandoned house in the countryside just outside of Berlin, in the shadow of an autobahn flyover. For months, he and Anashka had been talking about taking over the house and turning it into some kind of art space or music studio. Though nothing came of this intention, Mother D did drive Turner out to the house one unusually cold afternoon in early September. For Turner, whose mental state was most likely entering a stage of extreme deterioration, visiting the house was an experience of near-religious intensity. He had the sense of being in a place that existed outside of time, a primal, sacred and abyssal site, a 'portal onto infinity', where 'good and evil are one, are nothing.' While it is not clear whether Turner continued to visit the house after Mother D had revealed its location to him, his writing immediately became fixated on the image of a dilapidated house, unoccupied, on the fringes of a vast post-industrial city. In what has become unofficially known as the House Sequence, written in a frenzy of productivity throughout that September, the house is described as having cracked walls and smashed windows, and is overrun with weeds, yet radiates an intense, unearthly beauty. Across a broody strip of wasteland from the house, the broad, silent autobahn soars indifferently past, 'like mighty Quetzal-coatl.' In the opening variations of the sequence, the house stands serenely abandoned, crumbling and unwitnessed. Later, as the sequence gathers 'a kind of entropic momentum',[9] Turner begins to introduce human presences into the scene. One, two or, at most, three figures appear, always in the middle of the afternoon. They enter the house through the side or back door, which creaks on its hinges, and walk silently through the dilapidation. Various images occur and dissolve: a couple mutedly make love on the dusty floor; a man hangs a painting on a cracked, bare wall, and gazes at it for hours, tears running down his face (we never see what the picture represents); a solitary woman, clearly modelled on Anashka, enters a bedroom and lies on the damp floorboards where a bed might once have been. She lays there for a long time, gazing at the ceiling. She begins to masturbate, but stops before reaching orgasm. Darkness falls and still the woman has not moved. Suddenly we see her as a skeleton.

In the penultimate variation in the sequence, the house is the setting of a suicide. On a melancholy afternoon in autumn, a woman and a naked man watch in silence as a second man slits his wrists

9 Thomas Duddy, *Ecstatic Slaughter: Human Sacrifice in the Work of Georges Bataille and Killian Turner*, Radical Philosophy, Issue 116, Winter 1999

in the overgrown back garden. His body slumps to the ground and the man and woman stare at it for a long time (the moon rises, falls; the sun rises, falls). Then they leave. Finally, in what is both the termination of the House Sequence and the last of Killian Turner's known writings, a man arrives at the house, alone, holding a pile of photographs. He spends the night walking from room to room, weeping occasionally. In each room he stops and looks at some of the photographs, sometimes letting one fall to the floor, or placing one on a mantelpiece or windowsill. Very early in the morning, at the cusp of dawn, he leaves the house, gets into a red car which he has parked nearby, and drives away. The car merges with the autobahn that soars out and away from the city, towards an unknowable horizon.

The House Sequence was posted to Turner's publishers in mid-October. Near the end of that month, Killian Turner was reported as missing by his landlord. His rent had been due for three weeks. His apartment bore no suggestion that Turner had fled - the cupboard was reasonably well-stocked, his personal belongings had not been removed, etc. The West Berlin authorities interviewed acquaintances of Turner, along with residents of his apartment block. No one could say where he had gone, nor did they know of any friends or family of

Turner's who might be contacted in Ireland. After an examination of the diaries and notebooks found in his apartment, efforts were made to trace the individuals referred to as Mother D/Frank Lonely and Anashka. However, none of Turner's acquaintances were able to identify either of these from the descriptions given by the authorities. It appears that those involved in investigating Turner's disappearance reached the conclusion that neither Mother D nor Anashka really existed. Eventually, when several months had passed and nothing came up in the case, Killian Turner was officially declared a missing person by the West German authorities, and the whole affair was quickly forgotten.

Today, Killian Turner is remembered and read by but a few scattered devotees to the literature of collapse. Perhaps this is a fitting destiny for the man who declared, in a typically self-consuming aphorism, 'It is not enough to court extinction; *our* aspiration is *never to have been.*'

Killian Turner, c. 1984, Berlin Neukölln. Photo courtesy Sarah Flanagan

Disciple: *Oh enlightened Master, most illustrious and luminous Sage, oh Teller of wise and profound Truths, oh superior Mind that splits Diamonds and splits Hairs, oh Prophet, oh Seer, oh Saviour, is it really true, as the Thought has come to me in my Hours of Anguish, Despair and Gloom, when my Soul has craved, in its Urgency, some Glimmer of Solace – is it true, that, behind the apparent Veil of Multiplicity, Strife, and Separation, we are all, ultimately, One?*

Master: *Probably not.*

— Killian Turner, *Visions of Cosmic Squalor / The Upheaval*

In what has been called his 'suicide note' Killian Turner left detailed instructions, in the form of an annotated map of Berlin, detailing where and how to gather the materials that would make up his 'final literary work'. These materials included handwritten notes left in the apartments of four different friends and/or lovers (none of whom were acquainted with one another), several distinct lines of graffiti scrawled on the wall of holding Cell No. 3 in Polizeiabschnitt 22 in Charlottenburg, and sheafs of paper secreted inside various items that Turner had left on long-term deposit in an array of pawn shops all over West Berlin. Turner did not leave any indication as to how the pieces should be arranged, only that the work as a whole – however arranged – should be called *An Investigation Into My Own Disappearance.* In the instructions, Turner made it clear that the work comprised not only the texts found at the locations across Berlin, but the locations themselves, the efforts made to gather them, and any incidents, encounters or conversations that took place during this process. In January 1986, Turner's friend and former collaborator, the experimental poet Evelyn Miles, gained possession of the map and proceeded to gather the scraps and fragments it led to, eventually releasing the material to the Turner Archive in 2014. The arrangement below is the current editor's. It is not intended to be final or definitive. *An Investigation*

Into My Own Disappearance appears to have been composed in the months leading up to Turner's disappearance in October 1985 (therefore at approximately the same time as or slightly before the composition of the 'House Sequence'). Turner's mental state at the time of composition was thus one of extreme deterioration; there is evidence that Turner was convinced that the figments of his literary imagination were becoming real. As Thomas Duddy wrote in an essay on the convergences between the work of Turner and George Bataille published in *Radical Philosophy* in 1999: 'Given the troubling nature of Turner's visions, we might provisionally conclude that he killed himself out of moral duty, in order to prevent the terrible things he was writing about erupting into true existence.'

—*Editor's note, RD*

AN INVESTIGATION INTO MY OWN DISAPPEARANCE
Killian Turner

Q: What is the impossible task?
A: To be alive & dead. To be & not-be.

My First Born Bastard

Romy's one of those people who spends all week enthusiastically raping the planet, because that's her job, & discovers her feeling for the oppressed when she's pissed at the weekend. *But hell, we all have to earn a buck.* Bobby Sands. A hero & a poet. Which is meant to impress me because i am Irish, although i have gone off the IRA & don't believe in such a thing, in real life, as heroes. Or poets, or the Irish. Romy had, earlier on in the evening, when she was still struggling to repress her wish to be fucked, & in reference to a passing remark i had made about a recently deceased celebrity junkie, accused (accused?) me of 'casual cruelty'. Where did this casual cruelty stand in the hierarchy of cruelty as opposed to planting no-warning bombs in public houses, i inquired? She didn't or pretended she didn't hear or understand in the din of the mangled throng. In a world of no consequences &

no remorse & where i held absolute supremacy i'd
have fucked her & then poured petrol over her &
burnt her like a heretic or a witch or like Joan Of
Cock, revenging Birmingham. But i just fucked
her instead. On the floor, her skirt lifted, my pants
around my ankles. & afterwards, for days, i felt
that minor guilt, persistent under everything i did,
which i think i have picked-up like a mental dis-
ease from too many visits to cathedrals & librar-
ies. Why did i fuck someone i do not love? That i
hate, mildly - although this not make her special.
The ridiculous idea that i should marry her. A fully
formed, glowing, perfectly happy child romping
through summer meadows in my imagination
whenever i let my guard down. A child whom i
know or at least wish for its own sake cannot be
born.

The shit-eater Jingle

let's call it a dream, & not something i sing to myself about every morning in the shower, if there is
a shower. A toilet which flushes down into a dark
cage. In the cage are two naked men. Specially se-
lected from a whole army of captives, kept in a very
large cage somewhere off-track on a vast estate in
Bavaria. Two different naked men to shit on from a
height every couple of days. Until they drown in it

or die of disgust or the plague or whatever you die from eventually in such situations. The shower-song, which does not exist, & in any case is hardly a song, the little jingle say, the little jingle goes like this (*allegro andante*) 'oh who's a shit-eater, who's a shit-eater, who's a shit-eater today....' which is repeated until the end of the shower.

Phenakistoscope

the sense from the polizei the other night that they had captured an exotic non-native specimen. A specimen that had stepped through the TV screen out of a foreign, dubbed, made-for-TV movie, talking German in a voice not quite its own, lips not quite syncing. The one thing about being terribly intoxicated while under arrest is it doesn't hurt as much, although yes you wake up with bruises not knowing wherefore, like excellent sex. i have been arrested in daylight hours stone cold sober & i tell you it is no advantage to know you are being helplessly battered. The two uprights strained their gaze at me through a phenakistoscope in a 19th Century traveling fair. Two leery pigs out of a 1950's drive-in audience in the land of the hicks & the thicks - the appropriately credulous audience for such creations of the reactionary image-machine as *reefer madness* & *she shoulda said no* &

live fast die young. I think they believed they had captured James Dean or Jim Morrison. As soon as they slammed & ratcheted the cell door I lay on the floor & masturbated thinking of James Dean as two cops either end of me & then fell asleep.

From Holding Cell 3

chronic envy syndrome. A rhapsody.

the bell we couldn't lay hands on.

We seek to dream. We dream to seek.

The search for God is the production of God.

Perhaps a writer is one who can mirror the whole world,
and not commit suicide. Yet.

On the bridge

the real event will always disappoint because it has lost the sacred gleam of the imagined & foretold. Yet there are moments in many existences when the real gleams briefly ever so briefly with the rare & precious substance of the actualised foretold. It

is for presence at one of these exceptional, ephem-
eral moments of transfiguration that the human
being is seeking.

how he will get there

through the flashing, throbbing, blaring dark
dense street-draining mouth of a nightclub on
Winterfeldtplatz...

or down a disused manhole, the third one after
the Cafe Kranzler, two thirds covered with a century of hardened, mineralising crowshit...

or some circular submarine access secreted
in the labyrinth of pipes at the waterworks at
Beelitzhof...

or in the underground car park of the Universität der Künste, behind the student union
noticeboard...

or it will be a golden knob you turn half way up
the cone of the radio tower...

or it will be a screen made of water inside the
penthouse of the CEO, where there will be many
people in silken bathrobes, smoking...

What it is

Some will say warehouse. Stock control centre. Zoo of the damned, the circumstantially abandoned, the utterly owned, sold-before-birth. Those whom destiny, dark legate of time, hates most. Karma sink. Holocaust Continuation Project. Apocalypse Threshold. Rendering Unit. Sade's show-house. Santa-Never-Comes. Though deep underground, it is very bright. High roofed, as high as the Duomo of Florence, to accommodate the cages. Cages are piled upon cages to the height of the Duomo. Most stock can only be viewed by cranes. They are fed & hosed by crane also. They are not crowded, however. One per cage, 6 by 12. Cages all weaponised & electronically monitored. Communication between cages is punishable by summary execution by overwhelming electric shock.

Market Statistics

In this matter facts are difficult to accumulate. No specific accounting exists. A credible guess, after four years of study (those four years since *the suspicion* first gripped me), based on scattered police figures, articles in journals of radical sociology, UNESCO fact-files, sundry & often contradictory newspaper articles in various languages i can read or half-read, a good hundred ministerial dossiers.... indicates that between the Urals & the Azores, between Lapland & Gavdos, annually, *circa* 25,000 children under 16 go missing & are not found. These are drawn from the most miserable layers, the bulk being escapees/runaways from orphanages, foster homes, half-way houses & or juvenile detention centres of various sorts. The rest come from other forlorn demographics & the most downtrodden immigrant communities. Curiously, these children are always described as *escaped* or *absconded* but never as *kidnapped*. Rich children do not go missing. In a ten year period we are talking about quarter of a million children of misery. Distraught, crazy Berga, who made it over the wall & whose entire family have subsequently been arrested, says that children are worth 6 figure dollar sums on the east-west interblocular black market & that before she got over the wall she had been working on a case where a claim had been made that two children from an orphanage in Leipzig had been exchanged for seven 4-axis truck-loads of Levi 501s. Do the maths – a business worth 25 million a year if it can be imagined that the children are rounded up by the same 'company' & brought to market in the same way. & it can be imagined. I have imagined it.

Lakshmi Logic

Saw Lakshmi speak last night at the Freie Universität. At the end of her presentation she cleared her throat & asked everyone to leave except black women. i obliged as did all other non-black women in the audience. Was i the only one put in mind of the last time in Germany groups of people were segregated according to gender, race...? Horrid echoes. Lakshmi is not atypical of the international literati that are a kind of excrescence of the failure of '68 to make real change outside the university bubble. Her sentiments are noble, her poems atrocious. The Greeks had high sentiments, & great literature, & slaves who were not allowed to marry or to hold on to their children. It is not possible to make the recorded past nor the present cohere from a moral-aesthetic perspective. Only prehistory & the future, because they are entirely speculative realms, can be painted as morally just in the sense that the ones who produce the best art are the ones who deserve, by way of their exceptional suffering, to produce the best art. But let us imagine this to be the case in the present. Going by let's call it *Lakshmi Logic,* the million children kept in cages somewhere underneath Berlin would then be the greatest artists in existence -- & whoso believes in the transfiguring power of art, a power without the dream of which there can be no notion of art worth having, will be driven, at all costs, to witness this great work, even if it is only for a second or two before being shot or overwhelmingly electrocuted.

speaking out of the pain of having to live a difference that has no name says Lakshmi.

Why i must disappear

to render the impossible.

Gender & Race Neutral Story

Time vomited the market. The market attacked the boss. The boss disciplined the grown-up. The grown-up battered the child. The child bate the cat. The cat caught the rat. But the rat got away. Only the rat, only the rat, only the rat got away.

The other direction

Someone, apparently a man, was shot last night trying to get over the wall. First time in a couple of years. Radio now playing west-german border cop recording of the *grab vorfall*. Rifle Shots. Couple of cops or soldiers barking indecipherably as they approach. & then the guy, sounding cheerful believe it or not, *so you guys got me after all.* My thought: has anyone ever tried to get over the wall, which is also the wall between life & death for so many, in the other direction?

THE BALCONY, THE BLOG AND THE ETERNAL ROMANCE OF WAR
Alice Zeniter

I remember it was the summer of 2013. A friend told me about a friend of his who'd had a party on his balcony (a very private party) the week before, and about how he met the *strangest* guy there. He went on telling me about the dozens of people who stood all night long on the crowded balcony above the métro Couronnes; about a girl he would have liked to go home with; about the way Spritz has become fashionable everywhere even though it is disgusting. But he kept coming back to this figure he only described as the *strangest* guy. He emphasised the word 'strangest' in a way that ended up making me extremely irritated, though I couldn't explain why.

– Who the fuck was he? I asked, annoyed at him, and at myself for not being able to hide it better. (I've always thought my ability to hide my feelings was one of the qualities that ensured my everlasting friendships).

– I don't know, he said. Some literary critic.

– Oh, I said, suddenly interested. I had published a novel earlier that year and I wondered if my name might have come up in the conversation.

– He has a blog.

– Oh, I said again, far less interested now.

– Something with a Spanish name. Which is weird because the guy is not Spanish at all. I asked him why he chose this name, and he told me it was because of Bernanos. Which is even weirder.

– Why?

– 'Cause Bernanos is not Spanish either.

I sighed with an air of sophistication, of education. It was something I'd worked on a lot since arriving in Paris from my little country town, and realising I had an accent that betrayed my humble origins. Gradually I perfected an educated smile and an educated sigh that could help me get accepted without having to talk much.

– He went to Spain in the '30's, I said in my educated voice. This is when he wrote *Les grands cimetières sous la Lune.*

– Good title.

– Fuck yeah.

– Do you remember where he stayed?

– Palma de Majorque.

My friend beamed:

– That's it! That's the name of the blog.

– Bad title.

– I know. I kept thinking it was something like 'Vamos a la playa'.

We laughed, probably had a few more drinks, then I went home. Lying on my bed, I couldn't help having a quick look at the *strangest* guy's blog. On a website that was entirely black with white text, he professed his dislike for, well, pretty much every writer alive (or dead, as far as I could see). Even the most experimental writers, the ones I expected to be granted a reprieve, as they usually are when you encounter the 'I don't go for commercial literature' attitude, got nothing but scorn. And the blogger's scorn was of the flaming, scorching type. His only real love, he wrote, was Bernanos. He repeated this pretty much all over the blog. The Internet is full of haters having their rants. I wouldn't have been interested in reading for more than ten seconds if the guy hadn't had an impressive style, and a culture so wide and chaotic it was like being locked in a centrifuge with a torn encyclopaedia. He seemed to have read all the books that I pretended to have read - and the way he discussed them made me feel *good* about not having found the time (or courage) to read them. And so I kept reading about the blogger's exclusive love for Bernanos. And then, suddenly, he retracted another name from his list of scorn. 'Killian Turner', he wrote in one article, 'I could have seen as the *Renaissance* of literature, if drugs hadn't become such a part of his creative process. In his late Berlin years - the tiny cabal of Turner hagiographers will no doubt dispute me on this - he was nothing but the Muse of the substances he consumed.' (Although the website went down a year ago, I recorded some quotations from it in a notebook. The

52

rest I quote from memory and, as with a number of lines I've repeated through the years, they may have strayed somewhat from the original. I apologise for this.)

Amongst the many names I didn't recognise on the website, this one, Turner, caught my attention. Perhaps because I thought at first it referred to the painter, I looked for other entries and found a short article devoted to him.

'It is odd that Turner read so much of Georges Bataille,' Palma de Majorque wrote as an introduction, 'because Bataille is the least interesting entity one will encounter in all of literature, unless one is an anorexic girl dreaming of becoming a whore or a very pale boy dreaming of being tortured in an exotic Chinese way.'

He then started to explain that the writer disappeared in Berlin in the 1980s, a disappearance many were quick to conclude meant death, although it was clear that he, Palma de Majorque, wasn't among them. 'Because we like to think everything we read is addressed personally to us,' he wrote, 'we tend to see a writer's decision to quit writing (in such a drastic way that he almost quits *being*, too) as a spit in the face.' These lines were followed soon after by a quote from Turner, the only one in the article, the only words by Turner that I have ever read – and which I quoted afterwards in my fourth novel, *Juste avant l'oubli:*

It is not enough to court extinction: *our* aspiration is *never to have been.*

From there, Palma de Majorque jumped to Arthur Rimbaud's departure to Africa, away from poetry. Africa, he wrote, must be thought of as the opposite of poetry and not a continuation of it. And while discussing Rimbaud, de Majorque mentioned arms dealing, which brought him back to Bernanos and the Spanish Civil War, and to the core role of violence in what he called 'disturbing literature', or 'revealing literature', and then simply 'literature'. It was, the blogger assumed, the one thing that Turner missed that would have made him the Great Artist of His Times: a war. Travelling through continental Europe, he wrote, Turner was doing nothing but trying to find the wounds and scars of the last great war, but still that wasn't close enough. He should have enrolled to fight in Vietnam, de Majorque wrote in a very feverish part of the article, and then he would have achieved something to astound the ages. He quoted Matthieu Galley's diary from 1958 : 'Love, always love: the theme has worn out. Why didn't this horrific war in Algeria reveal a great poet? A Vigny? A Hugo? An Apollinaire... War is the only romantic inspiration that modernizes all the time. It would take no more than to go there, to create somehow a new metric, and to come back...'

I can only remember vaguely what followed. It is almost the last quote I recorded in my notebook. I know the article got back to Bernanos and attempted a daring comparison between God's place in his life and work, and drugs in Killian Turner's. The main idea was that it is impossible to write if you believe in the 'actual, dusty limits' of this world, yet drugs can only help you to push those limits so far because drugs are world-made, whereas God is supposed to be an outsider.

In the months that followed, my friend took me to his friend's flat and balcony, where he had met 'Palma de Majorque' (who, I would learn, was actually named Jean – but I didn't like his real name). I acted very friendly with the tenants, hoping I would be invited to their parties, which I was, eventually. But I never got to meet the *strangest* guy. I would like to think that I, too, witnessed a disappearance, but it is not true. It is just that, despite its 'actual, dusty limits', the city was too vast and its people too many for my purpose. Having realised this, I moved to the countryside and started writing a novel about the Algerian war, always wondering if Palma de Majorque's article had played a part in the genesis of my new work. I went back onto his blog a couple of times but nothing new was ever posted, and finally it went down. Flipping through my notebook, I sometimes pondered the final quote I recorded from Palma de Majorque, unable to decide whether it expressed real depth, or was merely the product of a shallow fever:

'Killian Turner is, to modern European literature, something like Shakespeare's sister for Virginia Woolf. No one can say that he was, nor that he wasn't, here. He is a promise of literature that it falls to us to keep – if we dare.'

Even the circus of assholes has a ringmaster.

—Killian Turner, *Visions of Cosmic Squalor / The Upheaval*

HOW TO DISAPPEAR
Professor Thomas Duddy

*'Dying is nothing. You have to know
how to disappear.'*
— Jean Baudrillard

There is a widely held assumption that, beyond the holy trinity of Joyce, Beckett and Flann O'Brien, and the work of a few less celebrated writers such as Aidan Higgins, Hillary McTaggart and Desmond Hogan, twentieth-century Irish fiction is parochial and bereft of experimentalism. Certainly, few of the great European avant-garde conflagrations ever gusted onto our shores. Yet, Killian Turner, an oddly neglected Irish author, has always struck me as an avant-garde unto himself. Despite Turner's bizarre disappearance in West Berlin in 1985, his unnerving sexual practices and political declarations, and the aura of uncanniness and genuine madness that permeates his life and *oeuvre*, Turner has accrued little of the fame attaching to comparably aberrant figures in the European anti-canon such as Artaud, Weil, Nietzsche and Bataille. (As my former student, Rob Doyle, points out in his welcome, if slightly hagiographical, reassessment of Turner first published in *The Moth* magazine, there is evidence indicating that Turner believed he was a reincarnation of Georges Bataille.)

Killian Turner's subterranean influence can be felt in the work of certain daring contemporary writers in Ireland and beyond - Dave Lordan, June Caldwell, Mike McCormack, Virginie Despentes and Alice Zeniter spring to mind. Artists working in non-literary fields have also found nourishment in Turner. His intellectual vitality has proved attractive to the discipline-hopping composer Jennifer Walshe, for instance, while the new wave of post-conceptual Irish artists currently shaking up the European scene have acknowledged his theoretical influence. Nevertheless, beyond this cult of admirers, Killian Turner remains largely forgotten. This very obscurity, however, seems appropriate in light of what I have elsewhere called Turner's 'poetics of disappearance', and the insistence running through his work that the true, far-reaching mission of literature (or 'the Colony', as he sometimes calls it), is to perpetrate its own extermination; that the writer 'should not be sun, but black hole, not the generator of meaning, but meaning's molester, finally its giddy assassin.'

In a sense, this book, and the exhibition of which it forms a part, does violence to Killian Turner by further restoring him to the visibility which he sought to evade. Despite our meddling, however, time will undoubtedly aid Turner in achieving the triumph towards which all his work, up to and including the notorious 'House Sequence', aspired: total and irrevocable disappearance.

"Development" you say?
Ruin-planting, more like.

—Killian Turner, *Erased Horizons, Forgotten Shores: Essays 1975—1982*

Killian Turner, c. 1984, Berlin Kreuzberg. Photo courtesy Sarah Flanagan

AN ATTEMPT AT A BIBLIOGRAPHY
OF KILLIAN TURNER'S
'MONK'S CELL' IN NEUKÖLLN
Sarah Flanagan

When you're in your twenties you live out many moments firmly in the present tense, and the cadence of your actions can go largely unheard. I left university at the age of twenty-three, and found that the sonorous aftereffects of academia followed me as I moved abroad, first to London and then to Paris. Finally I moved to Berlin, where I hoped to muffle the noise of stultifying learning once and for all. I'm talking about the burden of influence; about reattaining the vitality of naivety.

Of course, to say one once lived in the present tense is to admit retrospectively to some kind of lack. I had no grand plan. My parents were at a loss concerning my wilful desire to waste a perfectly middle-class upbringing and education. Telling them that I wanted to transmute my young life into poetry didn't help. Especially considering that I did not have such a whole lot of life to transmute in the first place.

Berlin, 1984. I spent a lot of time in the Staatsbibliothek; I spent every day in the Staatsbibliothek rather, from around ten in the morning until some time in the mid-afternoon. It was September when

I reached Berlin so it was getting colder and darker, and four months in it was too cold to really spend a lot of time anywhere else. All I could afford was a tiny room heated by an efficient dust-making coal oven that I was convinced was going to asphyxiate me with carbon monoxide. Outside, in the evenings the air grew thick with smog. Life was grey. My horizon was the edge of the page I was reading, at most the stack of books brought up from the library's own stacks. I would sigh as I paused a moment and looked at them all. I had no friends to speak of.

I was, and continue to be, happy that Wim Wenders made the Stabi library at Potsdamer Strasse such a central location in *Himmel Über Berlin,* because for me it was the location *par excellence* of West Berlin, and not Zoo Garten or the Dschungel Club or wherever else has been caught up in the nostalgia of Bowie and Nick Cave and Christiane Vera Felscherinow. The muted footsteps of scruffy, melancholic angels – this is how I remember that present-tense life of mine back then. It was anchored in the anechoic chamber of the library, of dictionaries and slow translation; it was full of Böll, Frisch, Grass – all these men – but also Plath and Angelou and Boland (my span of interest and attention made little sense at the time).

Until that is, I met Killian Turner. Then an uproar started.

I was introduced to the cacophony-maker by Martin Kluger, to whom Aidan Higgins had written me an introductory letter (it was all very formal and high blown, as I guess was still the norm in those days, like something out of a Henry James novel). When we first met for *Kaffee und Kuchen,* Kluger immediately started telling me how I absolutely had to meet the Irishman Killian Turner, a man of letters and a unique ambassador of everything and nothing, a curious case the likes of which many in West German literary circles had never come across before. Looking back I can see how it was: all these self important young men, or men in their 30s, condescending to a woman ten years their junior. But I wasn't complaining.

Turner was taciturn and distant – to say the least – but not at all unapproachable. He was generous, in his own way: I thought him the most eccentric person I had ever met. But that doesn't do it justice either, he was in those days (this is early 1985) set on a course below, or beyond, any and all social norms, and the rest of us were really just looking on as he disappeared, stepped outside of time itself. For instance, now that I think of it, he had a habit of turning his back on people as they entered the room, much like a shy child hiding behind the legs of his parents, and would only slowly reveal his profile before warming up enough to offer a very limp handshake and pinched-mouth acknowledgement. The claims that Killian was some kind of fervid woman-hater are dismayingly reductive. He was complicated, sure - who among us is not? - but he treated me with exquisite kindness and delicacy. I thought of him almost like a brother. I still do.

When I heard about Killian Turner's disappearance I immediately went to his flat in Neukölln. I remember leaving not one note but two: one under the door and another in his postbox. The former was personal and spoke about what he meant to me as a friend, while the latter was formal and stiff, enquiring of his health and whether he needed any assistance. Neukölln in those days was not somewhere one spent a lot of time: it had a kind of run-down, listless, end-of-the-road atmosphere, drab and derelict, and it took me quite some time to travel there. McGinley, the cultural attaché at the embassy, called me up to accompany him when the police arrived to enter the premises. I guess you could call it a date, an odd date, but that's how it was. The poor guy knew I was besotted with Turner in a way he had no way of describing or labelling, and so he figured this was as good a way as any to put Turner to rest. Really, I was curious to see what would be left of Turner and his meagre household.

I was lucky that the books came into my possession. There was nobody else to whom they could be bequeathed. I would be lying if I didn't say it was an uncanny feeling to receive the sole inheritance of someone of Turner's stature (as I saw it then). The books themselves were in a mixture of languages and genres (a dirty word for Turner), and I didn't really know what to do with many of them. Unable to read French, I merely looked them over and spent hours trying to decipher the marginalia that seemed like an artwork or a body of literature in itself. Even in the trashiest pulp-detective novel, Turner seemed to discern immense webs of appalling significance, 'the truth behind truths' as he sometimes called it.

Based on various requests from scholars and interested parties over the years, I have attempted several times at creating an exhaustive list of what these titles actually were - the books that Killian Turner amassed in his final home, in West Berlin. From memory, as well as my own intertextual analysis and notebook inspection, I believe I have come close enough - but who knows, really. Books come, books go. I ended up pawning off most of mine to a miserly book dealer just before leaving Berlin for good. The rest I simply left out on the street, *zu verschenken*... God knows where they ended up. No doubt some ended their days as the urinal for Hauptstraße's many stray dogs. I do not believe it is disrespectful to suggest that Killian Turner might even have wanted it that way.

Artaud, Antonin, *Héliogabale ou l'anarchiste couronné;* Gallimard, Paris, 1979.

Artaud, Antonin, *Oeuvres complètes, tome 1, livre 1;* Gallimard, Paris, 1976.

Baudelaire, Charles, *Paris Spleen,* trans. Louise Varèse, New Directions, 1970.

Baudelaire, Charles, *Twenty Prose Poems Of Baudelaire,* trans. ; Editions Poetry London, 1946.

Bataille, Georges, Gilles de Rais. *Leben und Prozeß eines Kindermörders;* Ullstein Taschenbuchvlg, Berlin, 1975.

Bataille, Georges, *Der heilige Eros (L'Erotisme). Mit einem Entwurf zu einem Schlußkapitel;* Ullstein, Berlin, 1979.

Bataille, Georges and Seabrook, W B, *Geheimnisvolles Haiti: Rätsel und Symbolik des Wodu-Kultes;* Matthes & Seitz, Berlin, 1982.

Beckett, Samuel, *Six Residua;* Calder Publications Limited, London, 1979.

Beckett, Samuel, *Molloy/Malone Dies/the Unnamable;* Calder Publications Limited, London, 1973.

Beckett, Samuel, *For to End Yet Again and Other Fizzles;* Calder Publications Limited, London, 1978.

Bloch, Irwan, *Sex Life In England;* Panurge Publications, New York, 1938.

Blanchot, Maurice, *L'instant de ma mort;* Gallimard, Paris, 1953.

Blanchot, Maurice, *Le pas au-delà;* Gallimard, Paris, 1973.

Blanchot, Maurice, *L'Écriture du désastre;* Gallimard, Paris, 1980.

Böll, Heinrich, *The Clown,* New American Library, New York, 1966.

Calvino, Italo, *The Baron in the Tree;* Harbrace Library Edition, London, 1977.

Celine, Louis-Ferdinand, *Death on the Installment Plan;* New Directions, New York, 1971

De Beauvoir, Simone, *Marquis De Sade: His Life and Works,* Castle Books, London, 1948.

Dick, Philip K., *Zeitlose Zeit,* trans. Tony Westermayr; Goldmann Verlag, Munich, 1984.

Erman, Adolf, *Life In Ancient Egypt,* trans. H. M. Tirard; Dover Publications Ltd., New York, 1971

Foucault, Michel, *Wahnsinn und Gesellschaft: Eine Geschichte des Wahns im Zeitalter der Vernunft;* Suhrkamp taschenbuch, Frankfurt Am Main, 1973.

Foucault, Michel, *Archäologie des Wissens,* Suhrkamp taschenbuch, Frankfurt Am Main, 1981.

Frisch, Max, *Homer Faber,* Suhrkamp Verlag, Frankfurt Am Main, 1977.

Genet, Jean, *The Thief's Journal,* trans. Bernard Frechtman; Penguin Books Ltd., Middlesex, 1965

Joyce, James, *Ulysses,* trans. Hans Wollschläger, Suhrkamp Verlag, Frankfurt Am Main, 1975.

Klossowski, Pierre, *Sprachen des Körpers: Marginalien zum Werk von Pierre Klossowski* (Internationaler Merve Diskurs); Pierre Klossowski, with Georges Bataille, Maurice Blanchot, Michel Butor, André Pieyre de Mandiargues, Gilles Deleuze, Michel Foucault, trans. Gabriele Ricke and Sigrid von Massenbach; Merve Verlag, Berlin, 1979.

Marquis De Sade, *Juliette,* trans. Austryn Wainhouse; Grove Press, New York, 1968.

Sartre, Jean-Paul, *Being and Nothingness,* trans. Hazel E. Barnes; Mathuen, 1976.

Simon, Claude, *Histoire;* Les Editions de Minuit, Paris, 1967.

Simon, Claude, *Le vent : Tentative de restitution d'un retable baroque;* Les Editions de Minuit, Paris, 1957

Simon, Claude, *Triptyque;* Les Editions de Minuit, Paris, 1973.

Weiss, Peter and Skelton, Geoffrey, *Peter Weiss' the Persecution and Assassination of Jean-Paul Marat As Performed by the Inmates of the Asylum of Charenton: Under the Direction of the Marquis De Sade;* Dramatic Publishing Co, Woodstock, 1964

Killian Turner, c. 1984, Berlin Neukölln. Photo courtesy Sarah Flanagan

For years I had been trying to think up stories, narratives, that would give me the excuse to convey, say, a deserted beach, because that – the beach – was what I really wanted to convey. Finally I thought, "Why not simply give them the deserted beach?"

— Killian Turner, from an interview with *ZG* magazine, 1981

CONTRIBUTORS

Professor Thomas Duddy is among the foremost experts on the life and work of Killian Turner. Duddy is professor of Comparative Literature at Goldsmiths College, London, where his courses include 'Literatures of the Missing: absence and disappearance in modernist and postmodernist writing'. Duddy has written extensively on modern European literature and contemporary art. His work on Killian Turner includes the papers 'Bludgeoning the Muse – the Transgressive Anti-Fiction of Killian Turner', and 'Ecstatic Slaughter: Human Sacrifice in the Work of Georges Bataille and Killian Turner'. Professor Duddy has described Turner's posthumously published collection of fragmentary writings, *Visions of Cosmic Squalor/ The Upheaval,* as one of the most significant literary-philosophical works of the twentieth century.

Sarah Flanagan was born in county Longford in 1961, and has won numerous international and national awards for her poetry, which has been translated into eighteen languages. Her first collection, *I Sensed That People Were Melting* was published by New Writers Press in 1978. Later collections included *Weapon; Rumours from Wannsee,* and *It's Better In the Dark* (for which she was awarded the

Rooney Prize for Irish Literature). She is the author of a novel, *Love in an Air Raid,* and has written numerous radio plays which have been performed on BBC and RTE radio. In 2001 she wrote a memoir of her years in Berlin, 'Vanishing City', which was published in *The Dublin Review,* and includes reflections on her friend Killian Turner. Since 2006 Flanagan has lived in Warsaw.

Having published five novels by the age of 31, **Alice Zeniter** is widely regarded as one of the most interesting voices among the new generation of French writers. Her books have won several awards (Prix du Livre Inter, prix Renaudot des lycées, prix Goncourt des lycéens, etc) and are translated into ten languages. Her most recent novel, *L' Are de perdre,* was shortlisted for the Prix Goncourt. Zeniter is interested in all forms of writing, including screenwriting, journalism and theatre. She dreams of writing the texts on the back of cereal boxes. She currently lives in Brittany, where she writes and works as the stage director of her own theatre company.

ADDITIONAL CURATORIAL
AND EDITORIAL WORK

Dave Lordan is one of Ireland's most lauded contemporary poets. His collections include *The Boy In the Ring, Invitation to a Sacrifice,* and *Lost Tribe of the Wicklow Mountains.* Lordan is also an essayist and short fiction writer, and is the author of the prose work *First Book of Frags,* as well as a collection of essays concerning literature and politics, *The Word in Flames.* He has been the guest editor of *The Stinging Fly* literary magazine, and was the editor of two anthologies of Irish writing, *Young Irelanders* and *New Planet Cabaret,* both published by New Island. He is well-known in Ireland's activist circles. Through his archival work, Lordan has been a key figure in the ongoing rehabilitation of Killian Turner as an avant garde writer of great importance.

John Holten is a writer and editor. Born in Ireland, he lived in Paris where he edited *To Warmann* by Djordje Bojic, before moving to Berlin. Interested in the history of recent European avant gardes, he has worked on the installation of Killian Turner's last known domicile. An occasional curator, he most recently he co-curated the exhibition about reading *Augury* at BQ Gallery, Berlin. Holten is the author of two novels, *The Readymades* and *Oslo, Norway.*

Irish words in my mind. Like sand in the wind,
a thousand miles from roaring water.

— Killian Turner, *Edge of Voices*

In This Skull Hotel Where I Never Sleep
Rob Doyle

A Broken Dimanche Press Publication
Berlin, Germany, 2018
www.brokendimanche.eu

Second edition

First published on the occasion of the exhibition
of the same name by Rob Doyle, at Büro BDP.
January 28–30, 2018 which was part of the series
a book, a room at Büro BDP.

Commissioning editor and curator: John Holten
Graphic design: Form und Konzept
Cover photo: Rob Doyle

ISBN: 978-3-943196-62-7

A number of these texts have appeared or will
appear elsewhere: 'Exiled in the Infinite – Killian
Turner, Ireland's Vanished literary outlaw'
was first published in This Is The Ritual,
Bloomsbury, 2016; 'An Investigation Into My own
Disappearance' appears in the anthology The
Other Irish Tradition, published by the Dalkey
Archive in 2018. An earlier version of 'How to
Disappear' was published under an alternative
title in Penduline (Portland).

With thanks to Zaza Burchuladze, and special
thanks to Dave Iordan for his archival and
curatorial help, without which this project
could not have taken flight.

Rob Doyle's first novel, *Here Are the Young Men,*
is published by Bloomsbury, and was chosen
as a book of the year by The Irish Times,
Sunday Times, Sunday Business Post, and
Independent. It is one of Hot Press magazine's
'20 Greatest Irish Novels since 1916', and
was shortlisted for the Irish Book Awards
Newcomer of the Year. Doyle's second book,
This Is the Ritual, was published in January 2016
(Bloomsbury / Lilliput), and was a book of the
year in the New Statesman, Sunday Times and
Irish Times. His fiction, essays, and criticism
have appeared in The Guardian, Observer,
Vice, Dublin Review, Irish Times, Sunday
Times, Sunday Business Post, Stinging Fly,
Gorse, Dalkey Archive's Best European Fiction
2016 and elsewhere. Rob Doyle is editor of the
Dalkey Archive's Anthology of Irish Literature,
due for publication in 2018.

Broken Dimanche Press
Büro BDP
Mareschstrasse 1
D-12055 Berlin